Merry Christmas 1993 Ca

Love

Based on the animated series "Babar"
A Nelvana-Ellipse Presentation
a Nelvana Production in Association with The Clifford Ross Company, Ltd

Based on characters created
by Jean and Laurent de Brunhoff

Based on a story by Elaine Waisglass
Image adaptation by Van Gool-Lefèvre-Loiseaux
Produced by Twin Books U.K. Ltd, London

This 1990 edition published by JellyBean Press,
distributed by Outlet Book Company, Inc.,
a Random House Company,
225 Park Avenue South
New York NY 10003

ISBN 0-517-051958

8 7 6 5 4 3 2 1

Printed and bound in Barcelona, Spain by Cronion, S.A.

BABAR

To Duet Or Not to Duet

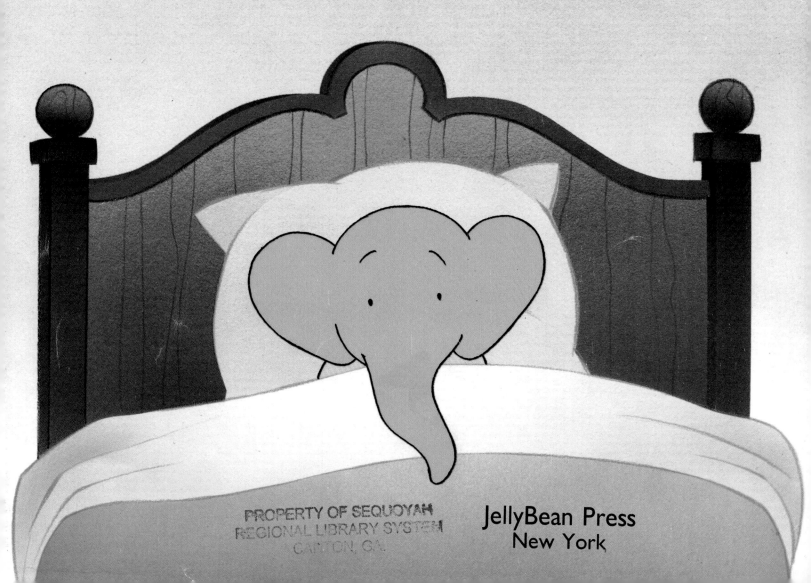

JellyBean Press
New York

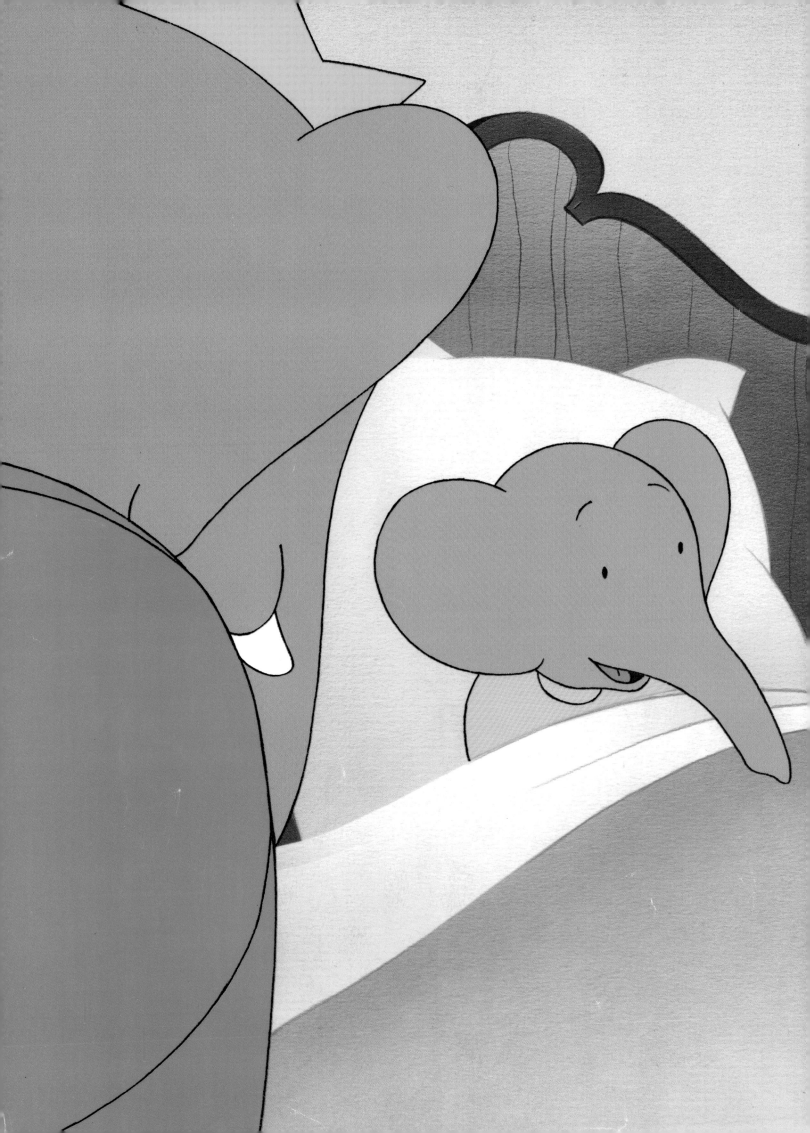

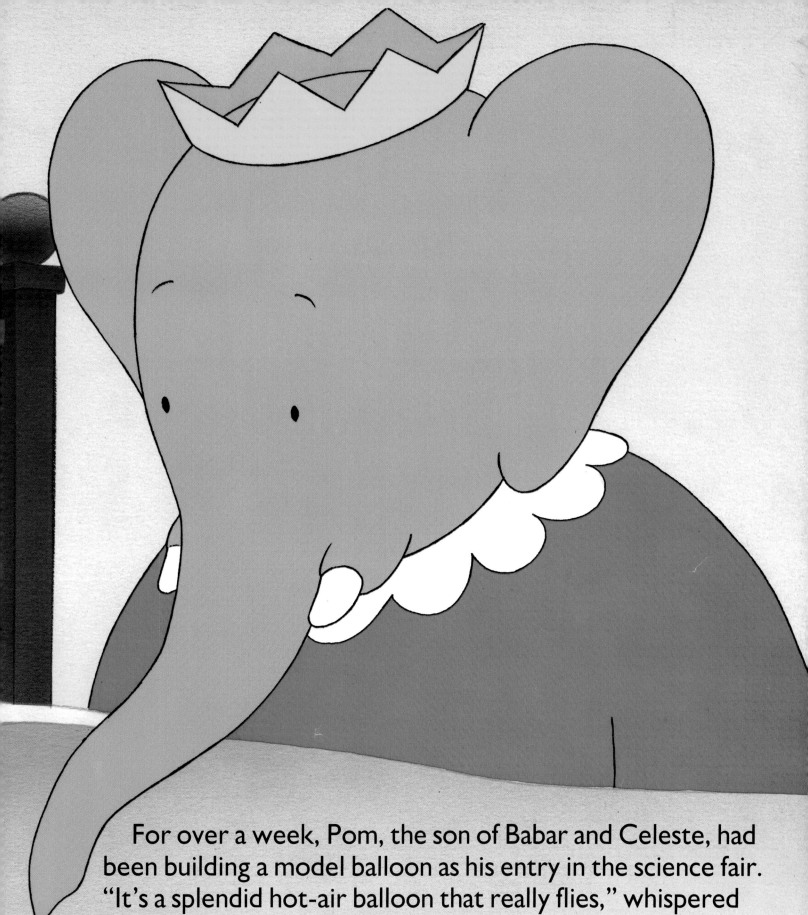

For over a week, Pom, the son of Babar and Celeste, had been building a model balloon as his entry in the science fair. "It's a splendid hot-air balloon that really flies," whispered everyone in the palace. Nobody had seen this model, but everyone was sure it would win first prize.

However, when the last day for entering the contest arrived, Pom suddenly went to bed with a mysterious fever. Babar, who was wise in the ways of his children, guessed that Pom wasn't really sick.

He remembered what he had been like as a child, and instead of scolding Pom, he told him a story.

"When I was only a little older than you are, a famous pianist, the Great Leopold, accepted an engagement to play a concert in Celesteville . . .

8

On such occasions, Babar usually made a short speech. Pompadour came to discuss the speech, but this time Babar said no.

The Old Lady—a fine pianist—had inspired him with a better idea. As a compliment to the Great Leopold, Babar wanted to play something himself.

"But one must study the piano for many years," objected Cornelius.

"At least play something simple," cautioned the Old Lady. "I could teach you a nursery rhyme, like *Frere Jacques*."

"No, thank you," said Babar. "I am going to play one of the Great Leopold's favorites: *Pictures at an Exhibition*." It was a very difficult piece.

But because Babar was the King, no one contradicted him. The Old Lady even arranged the music for him.

"This way, you will be able to play the keys using your trunk as well," she explained to him kindly. "It will be quite simple." Then she gave him a lesson. Her touch on the keys was as light as Babar's was heavy.

"Now, Babar," she said, "the real secret to learning the piano is to practice, practice, practice." And she left the room.

But as soon as she walked out the door, a miracle happened. Babar became a virtuoso, an expert, the king of pianists. With his trunk and his forefeet, he could play all the notes on the keyboard from high to low and back again.

He was even using his back feet! Dancing along the keys, right side up, upside down, and never, ever, missing a note.

Babar's two advisors, Cornelius and Pompadour, listened at the door with amazement. To play that well after only one lesson, they thought, was astonishing. So they believed that Babar could do what he had said he would: play *Pictures at an Exhibition*.

Unfortunately, Babar's new-found talent for the piano was just an illusion. The beautiful music they heard came from a record, which he had played on the stereo to give himself courage.

Before the record ended, Babar returned to earth. He knew he had a lot to learn, and he remembered the Old Lady's instructions, "Practice! Practice! Practice!" Music is not easy to learn, especially at the very beginning. But Cornelius and Pompadour were spreading the news of his remarkable talent throughout the palace, while Babar struggled with the score, unable to extract a true note from the wretched piano.

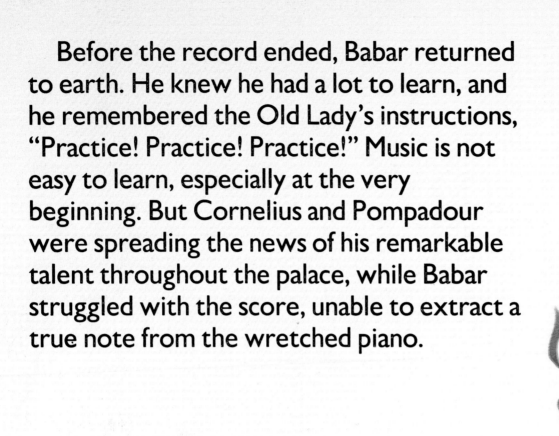

While he was struggling, over the keyboard, Babar looked out the window and saw Arthur, Zephir and Celeste, all with tennis rackets, walking toward the courts.

"Hey! Wait up!" he called. "You're not going to play tennis without me!"

Babar was sure he would feel better after some exercise. Closing the piano, he ran to join his friends on the tennis court. After all, music could wait for another day.

But the next day, even after some practice, everything was still disastrous. Babar played dominoes while the radio broadcast a musical program. Again everyone believed he was playing the piano.

When the Old Lady came in, Babar decided to tell her the truth. However, believing that he was making fabulous progress, she showed him the fingering of the first passage again—and left before Babar could explain.

24

The days passed. Each morning Babar would get ready to practice the piano. But each day, he found thousands of things to do instead, and by nightfall he had learned nothing! Babar tried to explain his problem to Cornelius, but the old general was unwilling to listen.

"Ah, Sire, may I present my compliments!"

"Oh, no! You are mistaken," Babar protested. "I haven't learned anything."

"And modest as well," said Cornelius, drowning out Babar. "No affectations, either."

What was Babar to do? He thought that a nice long drive might clear his head, and send him back to work refreshed. But who should he find waiting for him at the first crossroads, but Pompadour. He had some good news for Babar.

"The Great Leopold has heard about Your Majesty's remarkable talent for the piano and wishes to play a duet with you at the concert."

Babar was so shocked he was speechless.

That night, Babar had a nightmare! He dreamt he was alone on the stage, and the audience was waiting for him to play. But when he tried, all the notes flew away, and the people laughed and laughed. At the end, the piano turned into an enormous mouth with black-and-white teeth that tried to bite him!

Babar cried out and then woke up, safe and sound, in his own bed. But brave old Cornelius had heard his cry, and he came to the door to ask, "What has happened, Babar?"

"Oh, I just had a bad dream," he replied. "I think I'll have a glass of milk, and try to get back to sleep." Actually, this was the last thing he wanted to do, because he was afraid of dreaming about the dreadful piano. After ten glasses of milk, it was Cornelius who fell asleep.

Babar decided to get Pompadour up to help him stay awake.

"Please read me your new proposal on court etiquette, Pompadour," he requested.

"At this hour, Your Majesty? It's going to take some time."

"Exactly," said Babar. "Please read it now and out loud."

Unfortunately, the regulations were not very interesting. Poor Pompadour read all of them, and Babar slept like a log.

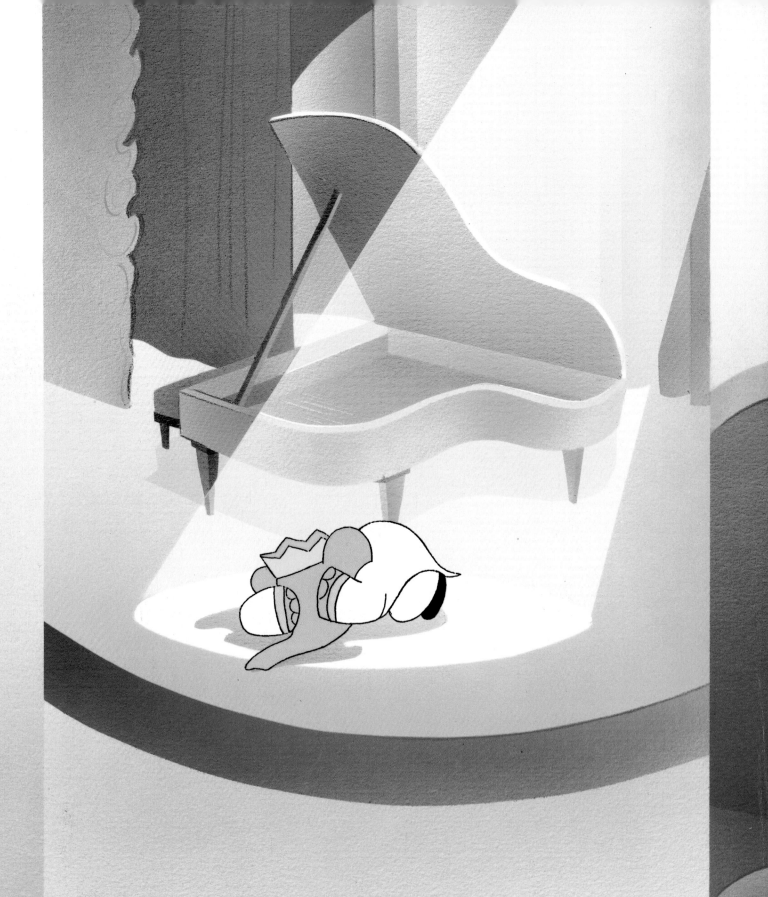

And just as he'd feared, of course, he had the same
nightmare, with the same hungry piano. But this time,
he didn't even try to play it. He just lay on the stage in
a tight ball and cried.

The harder Babar cried, the more the audience laughed and insulted him! "It's a shameful way to behave," said one. "An insult to pianists and elephants," said another. "We want our money back!"

"It's a scandalous way for a king to act," said a great voice. "Why don't we take away his crown, his title, his kingdom? Let's imprison him."

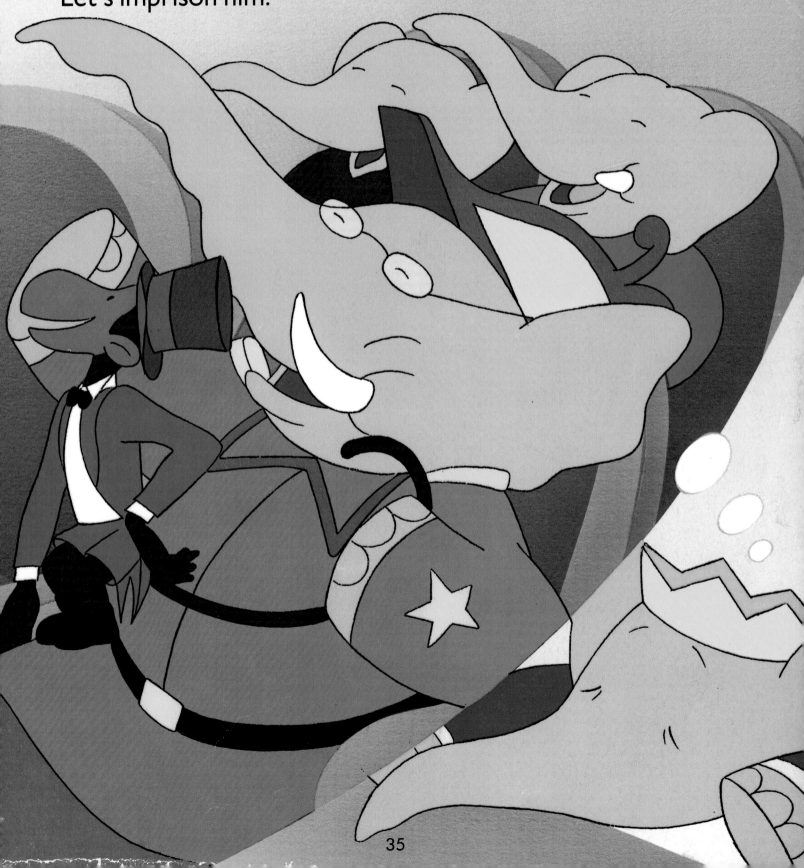

Fear woke Babar up. He jumped out of bed and ran at top speed to the Old Lady.

"Babar!" she cried. "What brings you here at this time of night?" Babar didn't stop to think—for the first time, he told the whole story.

"When you hear the music, it isn't me playing. It's a record, or the radio," Babar confessed. "Because I haven't learned to play anything! And I've told everybody I could do something I couldn't." He looked so sad, the Old Lady took pity on him and gave him a hug.

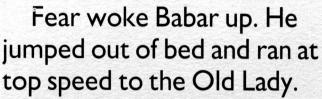

The day of the concert arrived. The Great Leopold was there. Everyone in the audience applauded when Pompadour introduced him, and they applauded after he played and when Babar took his bow as well. What had happened? What had the Old Lady managed to teach Babar in only two days?

Not everything, unfortunately. But she taught him to play the first few bars of *Baa, Baa, Black Sheep*, which are also the first few notes of Haydn's *Surprise Symphony*, the opening piece in the concert.

The Great Leopold played brilliantly, with variations and embellishments to every part of his program. When he finished, the dazzled audience gave him a standing ovation.

"So you see," concluded Babar, "not everyone has genius. But most people are happy to see a job well done. They appreciated the fact that I knew my limitations and didn't try to show off by playing a difficult piece badly. It was a hard lesson, but I promise you that after that I became more modest in my ambition. Don't you think that was a good idea, Pom?"

Pom had to agree. "It's like my balloon, Papa," he confessed sheepishly. "I wanted to do something important for the contest, so everyone would admire me. But I've only started the balloon. I think I'll be better off showing my rock collection."

"Good boy," replied Babar. "When do you want to do that?"

"Immediately!"

And the little rascal, now fully recovered, jumped into his father's arms.